Franklin
Giant Coloring and Activity Book

Franklin and Friends

© 2000 Modern Publishing
A Division of Unisystems, Inc.
New York, New York 10022

Printed in the U.S.A.
Series UPC # 49100

Franklin can count by twos and tie his shoes.

But Franklin is worried about the first day of school.

Beaver can read a book. Rabbit can write numbers.
What can Franklin do?

Franklin can draw! And he'll learn to do other things, too.

1=YELLOW

2=BROWN

3=GREEN

4=BLUE

1. COLOR SCHEME

Franklin knows his colors. Use the number code to finish the picture he made for his parents.

2. ARTIST AT WORK

Franklin is drawing a picture for Bear. He wants it to be perfect, so he's made four different versions. Can you find and circle what is changed in each one? Put a star next to the picture you think Bear will like best.

See Answers

Franklin is afraid to sleep in his shell
because it is dark inside!

1. THUNDERSTORMS   H.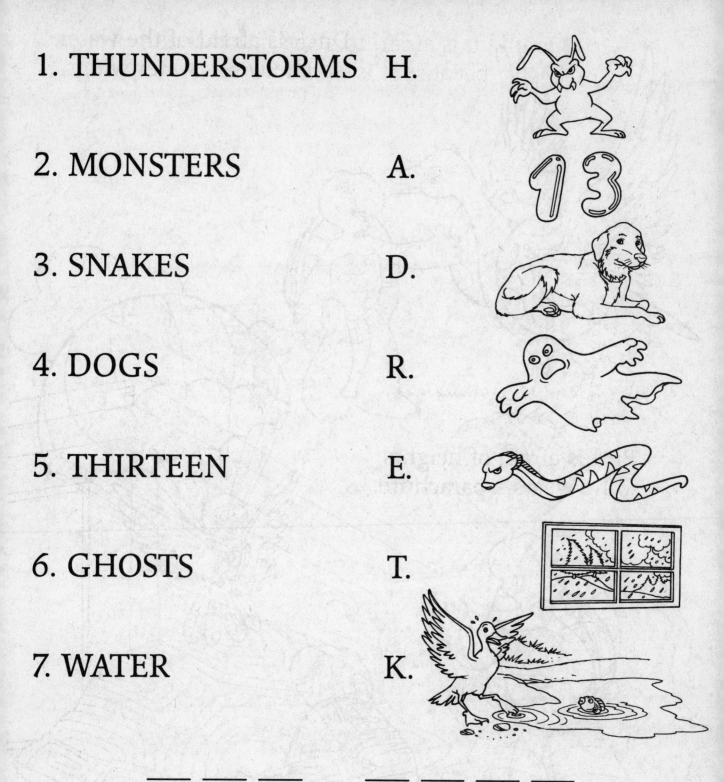

2. MONSTERS   A.

3. SNAKES   D.

4. DOGS   R.

5. THIRTEEN   E.

6. GHOSTS   T.

7. WATER   K.

___ ___ ___   ___ ___ ___ ___
 1   2   3   4   5   6   7

3. WHO'S AFRAID?

Look at the things some people are afraid of.
Match each word to its picture. Then write
the letters on the corresponding numbered blanks
to see what scares Franklin.

See Answers

Duck is afraid of the water,
so she wears water wings.

Bird is afraid of heights,
so he wears a parachute.

As he watches them,
Franklin gets a great idea!

__ __ __ __ __ __ __ __ __ __

4. GOOD NIGHT!

Franklin crawls inside his shell and turns on his bright idea!
Find the letters hidden in Franklin's shell. Look at
the letters above. Cross out the ones you found in
Franklin's shell to see his bright idea.

See Answers

BEAR'S TEAM 3
FRANKLIN'S TEAM 0

Franklin loves soccer, but his team never scores!

Franklin can't kick.

Beaver's tail gets in the way.

Rabbit has big feet.

Franklin has figured out a great play for his team!

Look closely at the picture.
Then turn the page to play a memory game.

5. GOAL!!

Franklin's team scores! Can you remember how the play worked? What did each player use to help score the goal?

See Answers

6. FRANKLIN AND FRIENDS

The words "Franklin" and "friends" start with the same sound: FR. What else do you see in the picture that starts with FR? There are four things!

See Answers

Franklin can walk to Bear's house and slide down a riverbank.
But he's not allowed to go into the woods alone.

Franklin's friends love hide-and-seek. Franklin is It!

7. READY OR NOT...

You're It! Fill in each space that has a leaf or berry to see who's hiding in this picture.

See Answers

Franklin has found everyone but Fox.
Fox must be in the woods....

8. LOST AND FOUND

Franklin is lost in the woods! Everybody is looking for him.
Follow the paths to see who will find him.

See Answers

Franklin promises never to go into the woods by himself again, no matter who hides there!

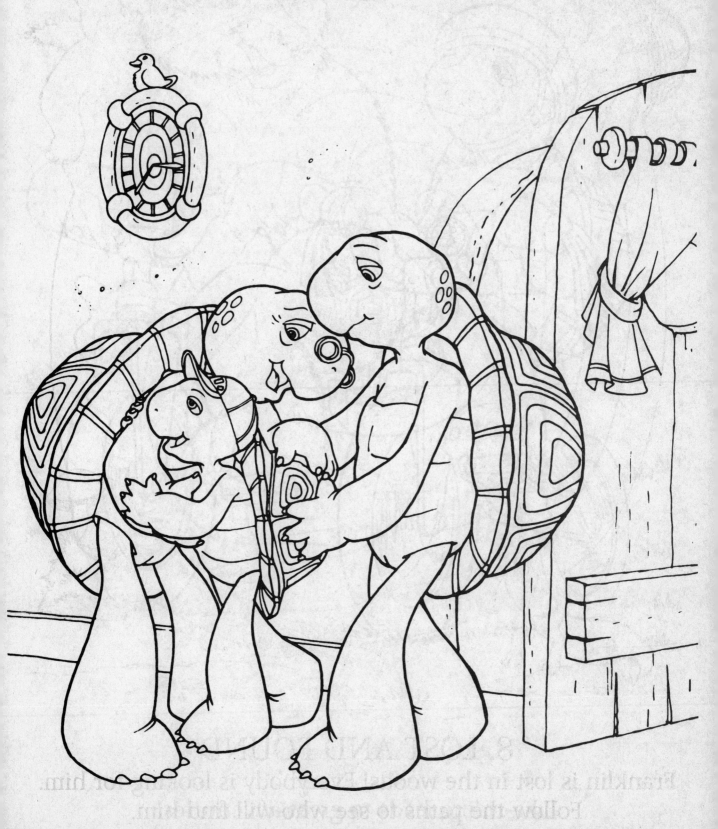

Bike-riding leads to great adventures!

.95¢

.50¢

.75¢

.85¢

.40¢

.15¢

$1.00

9. YARD SALE

Franklin wants a new ball, but his parents think
he has enough toys. He must buy it for himself.
He decides to sell some of his toys to get the money.
The ball costs $2.00. Circle three things Franklin can
sell to get enough money?

See Answers

Franklin's Traveling Magic Show

Franklin and Bear share a snack.

A. 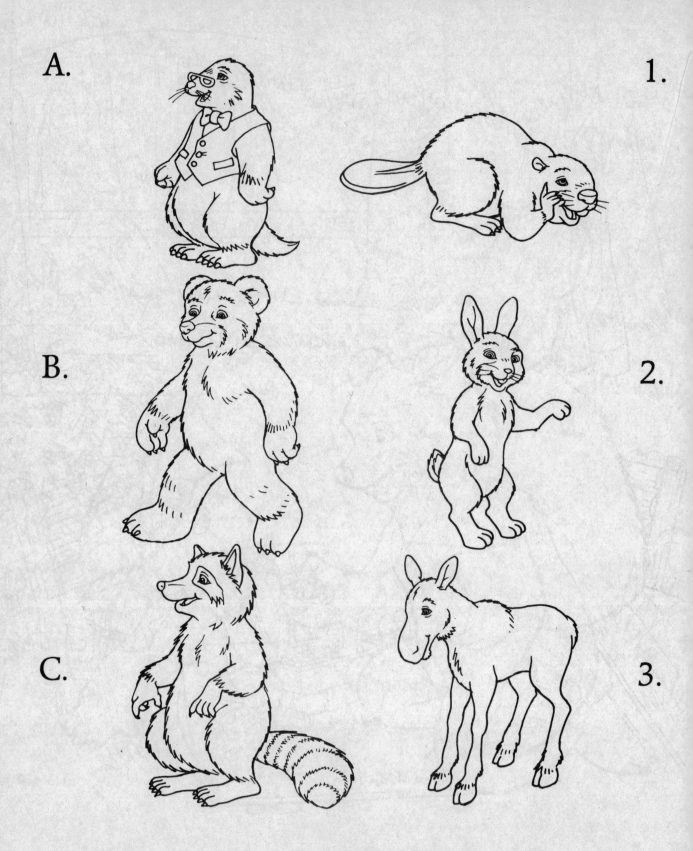 1.

B. 2.

C. 3.

10. LETTER FUN
Franklin knows his alphabet. Do you? Match the characters whose names start with the same letter.

See Answers

Rainy-day Fun

Franklin and his friends have fun at school
with their teacher, Mr. Owl.

Key: Write the first letter of the word for each picture in the blanks above.

11. SECRET CODE
Franklin is sending a secret message to Bear.
Use the key to see what it says.

See Answers

Knights and Ladies

Beaver's Birthday Bash

Go, Franklin!

A Sweet Treat

BEAVER

12. NAME GAME

Beaver's name contains all of the letters in the name of one of Franklin's other friends. Circle them. Can you make other words using the letters in BEAVER?

See Answers

Someone is moving into the neighborhood...someone HUGE!

Franklin has never seen a moose before and is frightened
of him. But Mr. Owl expects him to be Moose's buddy!

Moose wants to help Franklin design a poster for the class
bake sale. Franklin doesn't think he needs any help.

13. BIG TROUBLE

Moose is just too big! He's broken one of Franklin's favorite
things. Franklin knows Moose is sorry, but he's still upset.
To see what Moose broke, connect the dots that spell SORRY.

See Answers

Mr. Owl points out that it's Moose's first day in a new class
and he's probably scared, too. Franklin is puzzled.
How can anyone so big be scared?

Moose turns out to be a great helper with the poster
after all! Like Franklin, Moose is an artist.

14. POSTER PUZZLE

Franklin's design for the bake sale poster was good, but Moose helped make it even better! Look at the two posters. Can you see what Moose changed? Color it your favorite color.

See Answers

GMOIAONSET

15. GENTLE GIANT

Franklin learns that first impressions can be wrong.
Cross out the letters in GIANT to see the name of
Franklin's new friend.

See Answers

Franklin likes a good book.

Otter makes a splash!

Roughing It

16. BUSY BEAVER

Beaver has made up a new game. She wants to find
something in the woods that begins with each letter of her
name. Can you find them, too? Try this game in your room
with the letters in your name.

See Answers

Row, row, row your boat!

Franklin wants a scooter, but his parents say no.
He just got a bicycle. He doesn't need a scooter.

If Franklin really wants a scooter, he'll have to earn
the money to buy it. He says to Bear, "Let's sell lemonade!"

17. WHEN LIFE HANDS YOU LEMONS...

Franklin and Bear are making lemonade. Circle the things
on the counter that they won't need.

See Answers

Leap-turtle?

Franklin's mother wants him to clean up his room.

Franklin loves his old blue blanket.

Franklin's mother wants him to clean up his room.
He decides to do it later.

__ _ _ _ _ _

18. TRICKY TOYS

Franklin's friends want to play knights. Franklin can't find an important part of his armor. Find the letters hidden in the mess. Unscramble them on the lines above to see what Franklin needs. Can you find it for him?

See Answers

Franklin cleans up his room, and the missing sword appears! Being neat has its advantages.

The Neat Knight

Goose the Goaltender

Playing in the Park

Camping In

Building Blocks

Summer Sunshine

Winter Chills and Spills

IF FUN IS ALWAYS IN SEASON

Find the letters hidden in each seasonal picture.
Then unscramble them on the lines to see something
that's great about that time of year.

__ __ __ __ __ __

__ __ __ __ __ __

19. FUN IS ALWAYS IN SEASON
Find the letters hidden in each seasonal picture.
Then unscramble them on the lines to see something
that's great about that time of year.

See Answers

Having fun is the name of the game!

A Trip to the Museum

A Great Day for a Ball Game

20. TWO TO GO

Franklin can count by twos and tie his shoes.
Connect the dots, counting by twos to twenty,
to complete Franklin's new shoes.

See Answers

Franklin and Snail are making valentines for the class party.

21. GONE WITH THE WIND

Uh-oh! Franklin's on his way to the valentine party, but his valentines aren't. Can you see what's happening to them? Circle all ten.

See Answers

Franklin doesn't know what happened to his valentines!

Franklin feels so bad, he doesn't even want to get any valentines from his friends.

Franklin's friends know that he meant to give them cards.
They want him to have their cards, anyway.

Franklin still wants to give cards to his friends.
But he doesn't have time to make new cards today,
and tomorrow isn't Valentine's Day!

back   fold   front

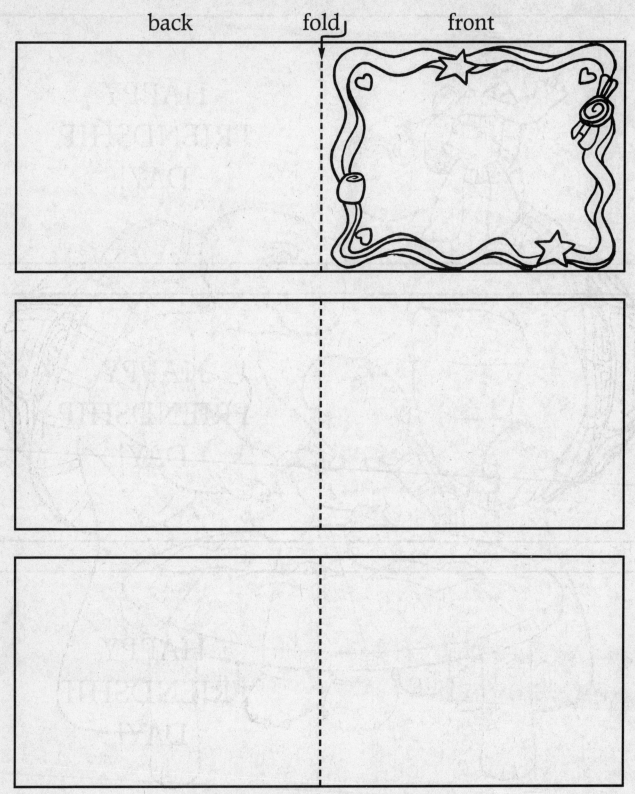

22. Friendship Fun

Any day can be Friendship Day. Decorate these cards
with pictures of you and your friends (turn the page
to decorate the insides). You can cut them out and
deliver them whenever you choose.

HAPPY
FRIENDSHIP
DAY!

HAPPY
FRIENDSHIP
DAY!

HAPPY
FRIENDSHIP
DAY!

Any day is a good day to be thankful for your friends.
Franklin's friendship cards are a huge success.
Mr. Owl officially declares it Friendship Day.

Bear sleeps over.

$$\overline{L} \ \overline{P} \ \overline{W} \ \overline{O} \ \overline{L} \ \overline{I} \qquad \overline{T} \ \overline{F} \ \overline{G} \ \overline{I} \ \overline{H}$$

23. SLUMBER PARTY
Unscramble the letters to see something fun to do at a slumber party. Then make your own list of activities.

See Answers

Paddling on the Pond

Take a Bow!

_ _ _ _ _ _   _ _ _ _ _ _

_ _ _ _ _ _ _

24. COSTUME PARTY

Franklin and two of his friends are all dressed up.
Do you know what they are? Write the words
for the costumes in the blanks.

See Answers

_ _ _ _ _ _ _

25. SOMETHING'S FISHY

Franklin loves to watch his pet fish, Goldie, swim in her bowl. Can you find all of the letters in her name hidden in the fish bowl? Write them on the lines above.

See Answers

ANSWERS

2.

3.

1. THUNDERSTORMS — H.
2. MONSTERS — A.
3. SNAKES — D.
4. DOGS — R.
5. THIRTEEN — E.
6. GHOSTS — T.
7. WATER — K.

$$\underset{1}{\underline{T}}\ \underset{2}{\underline{H}}\ \underset{3}{\underline{E}}\ \ \ \underset{4}{\underline{D}}\ \underset{5}{\underline{A}}\ \underset{6}{\underline{R}}\ \underset{7}{\underline{K}}$$

4.

N̶I̶G̶H̶T̶L̶I̶G̶H̶T̶

$\underline{N}\ \underline{I}\ \underline{G}\ \underline{H}\ \underline{T}\ \underline{L}\ \underline{I}\ \underline{G}\ \underline{H}\ \underline{T}$

5.

Rabbit used his foot.
Beaver used his tail.
Franklin used his head.

6.

7.

BEAR

8.

HIS PARENTS

9.

ANSWERS

10.

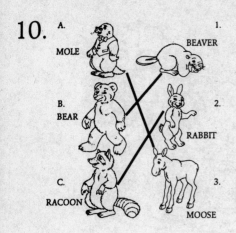

A. MOLE
B. BEAR
C. RACOON

1. BEAVER
2. RABBIT
3. MOOSE

14.

11.

15.

MOOSE

12.

16.

13.

17.

ANSWERS

18. <u>S W O R D</u>

19. <u>F L O W E R S</u>

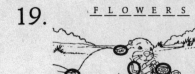

<u>S W I M M I N G</u>

<u>L E A V E S</u>

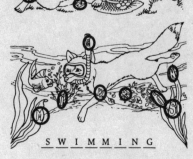

<u>S N O W</u>

20.

21.

23. <u>P I L L O W</u> <u>F I G H T</u>
L P W O L I   T F G I H

24.

<u>L A D Y</u>   <u>G H O S T</u>

<u>K N I G H T</u>

25. <u>G O L D I E</u>